for Janis

love --- pass it on and

best wishes for bliss

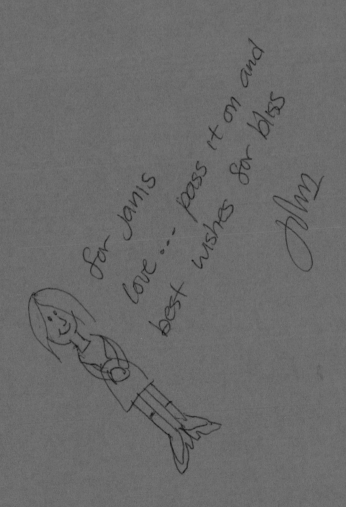

Thanks to:
Toni Markiet for her support and encouragement,
to Brendan and Josh for their inspiration,
and especially to my beautiful wife, Amy,
whose love made this book possible.

**SUPERDAN
RETURNING A LOST BABY
BRONTOSAURUS TO ITS MOTHER.**

**SUPERDAN
TEACHING TYRANNOSAURUS
HOW TO BRUSH HIS TEETH.**

**SUPERDAN CHANGING
HIS UNDERWEAR BEHIND
A SLEEPING TRICERATOPS.**

**SUPERDAN
DISCO DANCING
WITH AN IGUANODON.**

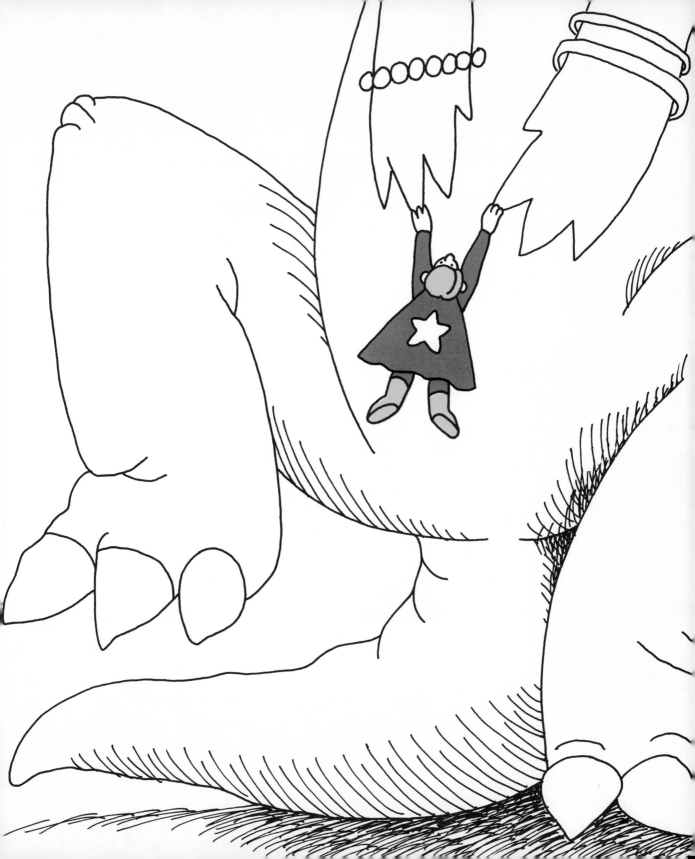

**SUPERDAN
TEACHING A CORYTHOSAURUS
HOW TO FLY.**

**SUPERDAN
TAKING OUT THE GARBAGE
AT THE DINOSAUR CLUB.**

SUPERDAN
TRAINING HIS DIPLODOCUS.

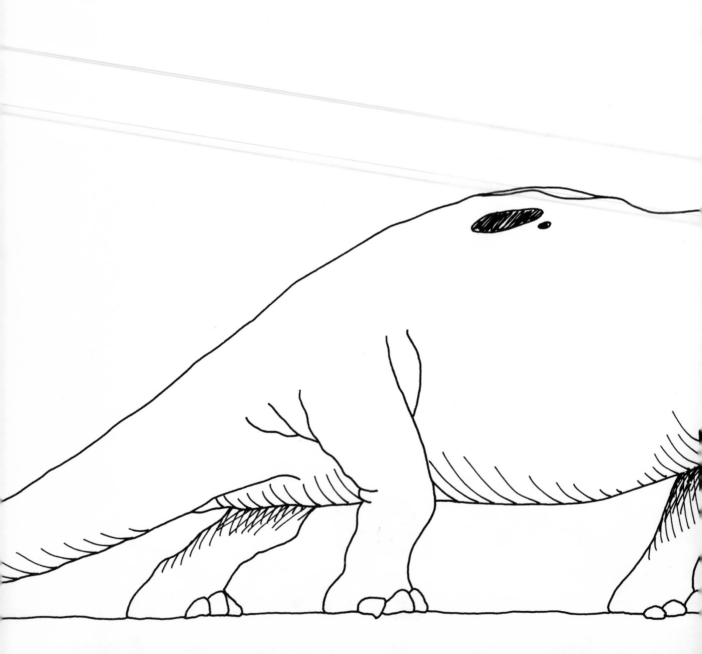

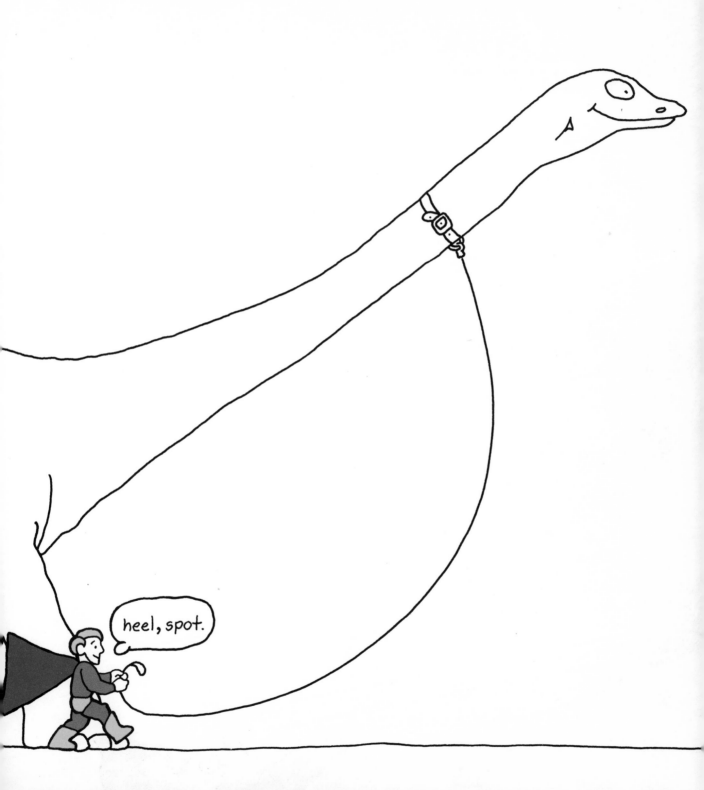

**TYRANNOSAURUS
PUTTING A BAND-AID
ON SUPERDAN'S FINGER.**

SUPERDAN
WASHING DINOSAUR DISHES.

**SUPERDAN
PUTTING NAIL POLISH
ON A BRONTOSAURUS.**

**SUPERDAN
TAKING DINOSAUR VITAMINS.**

**SUPERDAN
PLAYING TENNIS WEARING
DINOSAUR SNEAKERS.**

**SUPERDAN
PLAYING HIDE-AND-SEEK
WITH A STEGOSAURUS.**

**AFTER ALL THIS,
SUPERDAN WAS TIRED.
SO MAMA STEGOSAURUS
PUT HIM TO BED
AND READ HIM TO SLEEP.**

FOR BREAKFAST SUPERDAN
ATE A DINOSAUR DOUGHNUT.